ELIZABETH COLE

I Am Stronger
Than Anger

This book belongs to

....

....

The sun was shining and the clouds were blue.
So, little Nick and his parents went to the zoo.
«Wow!» Nick exclaimed, clapping his hands with glee,
When he spotted a koala up in a tree.

«Mom, I want that koala,» little Nick said.
But his mom said, "No," and shook her head.
«Honey, this koala has a mom and dad.
If we take it home, they will all be sad.»

«But I want it!» Nick stomped and started to shout.
He was angry and wanted to let it all out.
«I want that koala!» He was about to blow.
But, for the last time, his mother said, «NO!»

Then, Nick felt his heart beating hard and fast.
His brain felt like it was going to blast.
His throat tightened and his eyes filled with tears.
He began to flush from his toes to his ears.

Suddenly, little Nick heard a strange noise.
«Hey, psst, over here.» It was the monkey's voice.
«Why are you angry?» The monkey was curious.
"Cause I can't have a koala." Nick was furious.

«Hmm, I see.» The monkey was thinking in his cage.
«You have to learn to control your anger and rage.
There are many ways to get rid of anger, I know.
The first is to take a deep breath, and then slowly blow.»

Little Nick did what the monkey said.
He inflated his body from toes to head.
Then he slowly exhaled all the air he had.
«But, I still feel a little angry and sad.»

«Now, take a deep breath and count to ten.»
Little Nicky did it over and over again.
The monkey said, «You feel better now, I'll bet.»
Little Nick sighed because he was still upset.

Kangaroo

«When you feel angry, it's good to exercise,»
Kangaroo said with a gleam in his eyes.
«You can jump up and down, do sit-ups or squats.
That's how you'll get rid of your angry spots.»

Little Nick started exercising at the zoo.
«My anger is fading. What you said is true!»
«Shhh!» a voice said, «I'm trying to calm down here.»
Nick spotted the parrot, so he went nearer.

Clearly, the colorful parrot was furious.
«Why are you angry?» Nick asked. He was curious.
The parrot sighed deeply and this was his reply:
«My sister is sleeping in MY bed, I don't know why.»

«There are many ways to deal with anger, you see.
My favorite way is to count the leaves on a tree.
You can do anything that will make you feel better.
You can talk to someone or write an apology letter.»

«An apology letter?» Nicky widely opened his eyes.
The parrot continued; he sounded quite wise.
«Maybe you've been wrong. You need to think well
Instead of starting to blush, blow, and yell.»

Little Nick heeded the parrot's advice.
He thought about it well — not once, but twice.
«The koala is a wild creature and has a right
To be left alone, my mother was right!»

Little Nick took a deep breath and counted to ten.
He exercised over and over again.
No longer angry and with no reason to worry,
Little Nick went to his mom and said he was sorry.

Nick's mother noticed that he'd stopped shouting out loud.
She was surprised by his calm behavior; she was proud.
She hugged tightly and kissed her good little boy.
«Instead of a koala, I'll buy you a new toy.»

Expressing your anger in some ways can be bad
It upsets people and could make them mad
Don't allow your anger to ruin anyone's day.
Express it safely, in your own special way.

Go here to get your
bonus coloring page for FREE!

Dear Reader,

Thank you for purchasing my book!
I hope you enjoyed "I Am Stronger Than Anger".
I've put a lot of thought and love into this book while creating it.
It's a pleasure to inform you that this is just the first book of the "World of Emotions" series.

Frankly speaking, you are the reason why I am going to continue Nick's adventures.
I really hope that it will help your kids understand their feelings and emotions
and deal with them in a funny and exciting way.

So, please, tell me what you liked, what you loved, and even what you hated.
What kind of emotion would you like to see in my next book?

I'd love to hear from you. You can write me at elizabethcole.author@gmail.com

I would also greatly appreciate it if you could review my book.
Here is the link to "I Am Stronger Than Anger" on Amazon: amzn.to/3gfiXtS
Your input means a lot to me!

With love,
Elizabeth Cole

CPSIA information can be obtained
at www.ICGtesting.com
Printed in the USA
LVHW070739060722
722855LV00002B/3